Brady Brady
and the Santa Search

Written by Mary Shaw
Illustrated by Chuck Temple

Scholastic Canada Ltd.
Toronto   New York   London   Auckland   Sydney
Mexico City   New Delhi   Hong Kong   Buenos Aires

Scholastic Canada Ltd.
604 King Street West, Toronto, Ontario M5V 1E1, Canada

Scholastic Inc.
557 Broadway, New York, NY 10012, USA

Scholastic Australia Pty Limited
PO Box 579, Gosford, NSW 2250, Australia

Scholastic New Zealand Limited
Private Bag 94407, Botany, Manukau 2163, New Zealand

Scholastic Children's Books
Euston House, 24 Eversholt Street, London NW1 1DB, UK

www.scholastic.ca

Library and Archives Canada Cataloguing in Publication

Title: Brady Brady and the Santa search / written by Mary Shaw ;
illustrated by Chuck Temple.

Names: Shaw, Mary, 1965- author. | Temple, Chuck, 1962- illustrator.

Description: Series statement: Brady Brady

Identifiers: Canadiana 20200220934 | ISBN 9781443175524 (hardcover) | ISBN
9781443175548 (softcover)

Classification: LCC PS8587.H3473 B735 2021 | DDC jC813/.6

6 5 4 3 2 1   Printed in China 62   21 22 23 24 25

To one of my biggest fans, my uncle, Reverend Ron Cote.
Thank you for telling everyone you know about the Brady Brady books.
— Mary Shaw

To Cara, Andrew, and Tom.
The bright lights of Christmases to come.
— Chuck Temple

Brady loved hockey. Brady also loved Christmas.

These days, hockey and Christmas were all Brady thought about. His family had to call him twice to get his attention.

"Brady, Brady, that's enough tinsel!"
"Brady, Brady, leave those cookies!"
"Brady, Brady, go to bed!"

Brady's team, the Icehogs, had a game on Christmas Eve. As usual, Brady was the first one at the rink so he could high-five his teammates as they arrived. The kids chatted excitedly about what they had asked Santa for.

Brady fell silent. He had written a letter to Santa asking for a big red metal hockey net, but he had forgotten to mail it. And now it was Christmas Eve. How could he tell Santa what he wanted? Was it too late?

Brady was so worried he didn't yell the
team cheer as loudly as he usually did.

"We've got the power,
We've got the might,
Santa is a hockey fan,
And he'll be busy tonight!"

The ref blew his whistle and the game began.
Brady couldn't stop thinking about his letter to Santa.

It bothered him so much he skated right into
Tes in the middle of her "Twirlin' Torpedo."

The score was tied with only ten seconds remaining when Brady got a breakaway.

Brady could hear the cheering as he skated toward the net. It made him skate even faster.

Brady knew he would do his go-to move, where he would fake a shot, then slide the puck into the five-hole between the goalie's pads.

But just as Brady was about to shoot, someone at the corner of the glass caught his eye.

Brady's jaw dropped when he realized who it was.

Tripping over his stick, he slid right past the net as the final buzzer went off.

Brady scrambled to his feet and looked over to the corner, but there was nobody at the glass. He raced to his bench.

"Did you see him? Did you see him?" Brady shouted breathlessly.

The Icehogs looked confused.

"See who?" Tes asked.

"SANTA!!!" Brady screamed, pointing to the far corner. "Santa was watching our game! And I *NEED* to find him. I forgot to send him my letter. He won't know what I'm hoping for."

The Icehogs rushed to the dressing room and took off their skates. Brady led them to the corner of the glass where he had seen Santa cheering him on.

But there was nobody there.

Brady turned to face his teammates.

"I'm telling you, he was **right here**,"
Brady explained, pointing to a smudge on
the glass. The kids stared, wide-eyed.

"Look at this!" Tree said, as he bent over to pick up a candy cane.

"There's another one over here!" yelled Tes.

"He's here **somewhere**," insisted Brady.

The search was on.

"This must be from his sleigh," sang Tree, pointing to a metal blade tucked under the bleachers.

At the concession stand, they found a red hat.
"Santa must have lost it," suggested Caroline.

Behind the arena, they found prints in the snow.
"For sure, these are from a reindeer," squealed Gregory.

And when they heard bells ringing, they rushed back into the rink.

But Santa was nowhere to be found.

Disappointed, the Icehogs walked back to their dressing room to take off the rest of their equipment.

Brady slumped in the corner and groaned, "How is Santa going to know?"

On his way out of the rink, Brady pressed his hand to the smudge on the glass and blinked back a tear.

Brady cheered up a little when they
pulled into the driveway and he saw his
great rink all lit up. It looked magical.

Skating on his backyard rink with his family
was Brady's favorite Christmas Eve tradition.

"Put those skates back on," said Grandpa.
"It's time for a little holiday hockey."

Brady shrugged, but he laced up his skates.

Brady's whole family played for hours. It had just started snowing when Brady's mother brought out cocoa. "Time to come in," she said.

Brady let out a little sigh. Even with his old net, his backyard rink was still the best ever. Snowflakes melted on his face as he looked up to the sky.

"Wait! I have a great idea!" Brady shouted.

Grabbing a squirt bottle full of juice, Brady wrote in big letters across his rink:

Hi Santa. Can you please leave me a new hockey net? Thank you. Safe travels!

When Mom insisted it was time for bed,
Brady set out milk and cookies for Santa
— and carrots for the reindeer, of course!

His Granpa tucked him in and read *'Twas the Night Before Christmas*. Brady drifted off to sleep dreaming about big goals and flying reindeer.

Early the next morning, Brady ran from bedroom to bedroom waking everyone up. He slid down the stairs and rushed to the tree. And there, on his brand new hockey net, was a note:

I would have shot the puck top corner on that breakaway.
Merry Merry Christmas Brady Brady

Love, Santa